THE AMAZING ADVENTURES OF THE SUPER-PETS!™

Crime-fighting Cat!

by Steve Korté

illustrated by Art Baltazar

Supergirl based on characters
created by Jerry Siegel and Joe Shuster
by special arrangement with the
Jerry Siegel Family

Raintree is an imprint of Capstone Global Library Limited, a company incorporated in England and Wales having its registered office at 264 Banbury Road, Oxford, OX2 7DY – Registered company number: 6695582
www.raintree.co.uk
myorders@raintree.co.uk

978 1 3982 0618 2

British Library Cataloguing in Publication Data
A full catalogue record for this book is available from the British Library.

Designed by Ted Williams
Design Elements by Shutterstock/SilverCircle

Printed and bound in the United Kingdom

CONTENTS

He is Supergirl's
furry friend.

He was once an ordinary cat.

He now has many
of the same superpowers
as Supergirl.

These are . . .

THE AMAZING ADVENTURES OF

Streaky the Super-Cat!

CHAPTER 1

Harbour rescue

It's a beautiful, sunny day in Midvale.

Supergirl zooms through the clear, blue

sky. People in the harbour below wave.

Her fuzzy orange Super-Cat, Streaky,

flies alongside her.

Just then, something surprising happens.

From below, a submarine bursts out of

the water. It flies towards them!

WHOOSH!

Supergirl and Streaky see a small

aeroplane falling through the air. The

plane is headed straight for the harbour!

Supergirl knows that she can't save both the submarine and the aeroplane at the same time.

"Streaky, it's time for teamwork," says Supergirl.

Supergirl grabs the submarine. She pushes it back into the sea.

Streaky uses super-strong paws to guide the aeroplane safely to the ground.

Under the sea

Under the water, the Super Hero team discovers another surprise.

It's Mr Mxyzptlk, the trouble-making imp from another world! He uses magic for mischief. He must have sent the plane and the sub.

There is only one way to get

Mr Mxyzptlk to leave Earth. He has to be

tricked into saying his name backwards.

Supergirl has an idea. She uses heat vision from her eyes to burn the word "Kltpzyxm" onto the side of the sub.

Supergirl points to the submarine.

Mr Mxyzptlk starts to read. But he

only manages to get out "Kltp . . . "

before he swallows water. He can't say

the whole word out loud while he's

underwater.

Mr Mxyzptlk waves. Then he's gone!

CHAPTER 3

A talking cat!?

Supergirl and Streaky soon discover the imp's next bit of mischief.

All of the animals in Midvale are talking!

Dogs are asking their owners for longer walks. The elephants in the zoo are demanding more peanuts.

Even Streaky can talk! "How about

sushi for lunch?" he suggests.

"First we need to deal with Mxy," says

Supergirl. "I have an idea. I'm going to

need your help."

"Then we can get sushi!" adds

Streaky. "Extra tuna, please."

A few hours later, Streaky is sitting on a park bench.

The Super-Cat is holding the Midvale newspaper in his paws.

Mr Mxyzptlk flies nearby and stares at Streaky.

"What are you doing?" asks Mxy.

Streaky replies, "I can speak. But I can't read. There is a story on the front page with a large picture of you. I don't know what it says."

Mr Mxyzptlk grabs the newspaper.

"A story about me?" he asks with excitement.

He reads the story out loud to Streaky.

"Mr Kltpzyxm is causing mayhem in Midvale," he says.

A frown fills his face. He has been tricked into saying his name backwards!

Mr Mxyzptlk disappears in a cloud of pink smoke.

Supergirl arrives and smiles at Streaky.

"Great teamwork, Streaky!" says Supergirl. "Our fake newspaper for Mxy worked!"

Streaky opens his mouth to agree. But he is only able to say, "Meow!"

Streaky and all the other animals in Midvale are back to normal.

Fortunately, Supergirl doesn't need words to know that Streaky is a happy Super-Cat.

Streaky purrs loudly as he and Supergirl

cuddle and enjoy sushi together on

the bench.

AUTHOR!

Steve Korté is the author of many books for children and young adults. He worked at DC Comics for many years, editing more than 600 books about Superman, Batman, Wonder Woman and the other heroes and villains in the DC Universe. He lives in New York City, USA, with his husband, Bill, and their super-cat, Duke.

ILLUSTRATOR!

Famous cartoonist Art Baltazar is the creative force behind *The New York Times* bestselling, Eisner Award-winning DC Comics' Tiny Titans; co-writer for Billy Batson and the Magic of Shazam, Young Justice, Green Lantern Animated (Comic); and artist/co-writer for the awesome Tiny Titans/Little Archie crossover, Superman Family Adventures, Super Powers, and Itty Bitty Hellboy! Art is one of the founders of Aw Yeah Comics comic shop and the ongoing comic series! Aw yeah, living the dream! He stays home and draws comics and never has to leave the house! He lives with his lovely wife, Rose, sons Sonny and Gordon and daughter Audrey! AW YEAH MAN! Visit him at www.artbaltazar.com

"Word power"

harbour a place where ships load and unload their supplies

imp a small creature that plays harmful tricks

mayhem violent or damaging behaviour

mischief playfulness that creates trouble

Mxyzptlk a creature from another world who likes to play tricks on others

submarine a ship that can travel both on the surface of and under the water

sushi a meal made of vegetables, raw fish and cold, cooked rice

WRITING PROMPTS

1. Imagine you were at the zoo the day the animals started to talk! Write about it as though you were a newspaper reporter.

2. Mr Mxyzptlk is a real troublemaker! Write another story featuring the magical imp.

3. Do you think the people riding in the submarine and the aeroplane were scared? Describe what their day might have been like.

DISCUSSION QUESTIONS

1. Mr Mxyzptlk has to be tricked into saying his name backwards. How would you do it?

2. Streaky and the other animals in Midvale are given the ability to talk. What do you think your pet would say to you? If you haven't got a pet, think of something an animal on the street or at the zoo might talk about.

3. Think of a time you have had to use teamwork. What were the benefits? What could have gone better?